Artlist Collection
THE D

Lab to the Rescue!

By Howie Dewin

SCHOLASTIC INC.

New York   Toronto   London   Auckland   Sydney
Mexico City   New Delhi   Hong Kong   Buenos Aires

For Hap and the Min who loved her

ISBN-13: 978-0-545-10484-5
ISBN-10: 0-545-10484-X

© 2009 artlist

Published by Scholastic Inc. All rights reserved.
SCHOLASTIC and associated logos are trademarks and/or registered trademarks of Scholastic Inc.

12 11 10 9 8 7 6 5 4 3 2 1   9 10 11 12 13/0

Designed by Deena Fleming
Printed in the U.S.A.
First printing, March 2009

Meet Hap.

Hap is a Labrador Retriever. She used to live in a big house.

Then her family decided to move to California. They would fly there. But Hap would travel in a van. Her family would stop in several cities, so Hap couldn't go with them. They would meet again in just a week. . . .

That was before the back door of the van opened in the desert. Before Hap's crate slipped out as the van sped away.

Now Hap doesn't belong to anyone. . . .

Chapter 1

Hap ran fast. She had to find a place to hide. In her mouth was a beefsteak.

Boy, did I get lucky! thought Hap.

She had found the steak in a restaurant's garbage can. Hap had dug in that garbage every night. Usually, she found only a stale roll. But tonight she found an entire steak!

The taste made her drool. She was so hungry. But she couldn't stop to eat until she was sure no one could see her.

It was hard to think of herself as a stray. She knew that many people didn't like stray dogs. She had to be careful that no one saw her.

But there was something else to avoid: Lobo the wolf.

Lobo was the leader of a wolf pack. The first time Hap saw him was on the night she had been lost. She had been hiding behind a tumbleweed. Four other wolves followed Lobo. He howled fiercely at the moon. Then he turned to the other wolves.

"You call yourselves wolves?" said Lobo. "Not one of you is tough enough! It's time you proved your worth!"

The other wolves looked scared.

"In the next four days, I am ordering each of you to lead the hunt. You must each show up with some food. AND," he shouted, "I will eat first!"

Hap was frightened. She'd never seen a meaner creature in her life.

Hap spotted the wolves many times after that. Luckily, she was always able to hide. Every time, they were attacking an animal or stealing food.

I've heard that all dogs descended from wolves, Hap thought. *But I hope they aren't all as mean as Lobo.*

Hap was starving. The taste of steak made her even hungrier.

Wolves and Dogs

Scientists believe that all dogs descended from wolves. In fact, some say that dogs evolved from a small number of wolves who lived with humans near China about 15,000 years ago. Why are there so many different kinds of dogs today? For thousands of years, people have been breeding dogs to develop all different sizes, shapes, and talents.

She glanced from side to side. She spotted a wide cactus and ducked behind it. It was perfect! She turned in a circle three times like she was getting ready to sleep. At last, she was ready to eat her wonderful dinner!

The first bite was the best thing Hap had ever tasted.

I never knew steak was so amazing! Hap thought.

CRACKLE!

Hap froze.

What was that? she wondered. She tried to believe she hadn't heard anything—

SNAP!

She tried to look around. Ten glowing eyes stared at her from the darkness.

It was Lobo. Lobo and the four other wolves.

"We have someone new in town," said Lobo. He laughed cruelly.

Hap's mind was blank. She could not think.

Lobo stepped toward her.

"Boys," cackled Lobo, "I think our new

friend has brought us dinner."

Hap lifted the steak in her mouth and gave a low growl. She didn't mean to growl. She knew that Lobo could kill her. But she wouldn't give up her only food!

Lobo and the wolves took another step. Hap's mind flooded with pictures. She saw herself sitting in her old living room. She remembered the three kids who used to play with her.

Then she ran.

"Get her!" Lobo shouted. Hap heard wolf paws running behind her.

I have to get to town, thought Hap. *They wouldn't dare follow me there!*

The wolves were close behind. She had to run faster!

Chapter 2

Hap could still feel the heat of the wolf pack behind her.

She was losing ground. Soon they would nab her. Then, in the distance, she saw the small twinkling lights of town.

Someone yelped behind her. She barreled ahead. The town lights grew brighter. The pounding paws behind her quieted. Hap was afraid to turn her head.

"I will get you, you yellow-bellied lightweight!" Lobo called.

Hap slowed down. Lobo's voice was far away. She had outrun them! They wouldn't dare follow her into town.

Hap stared back at Lobo. The other wolves were trotting away. But Lobo stared at Hap. Even from far away, Hap could feel the danger in Lobo's glare. Then, without a word, Lobo also went away.

"I beat a pack of wolves!" Hap cried out. She was shaking like a leaf. But she'd saved herself. It was terrifying. But it was exciting, too.

"Hey, yellow-belly!" Lobo's voice called from the darkness. "Thanks for the dinner!"

Suddenly, Hap realized that her mouth was empty. She had dropped the steak. She didn't remember dropping it. But her mouth was empty.

"AH-OOOOOOOO!" She heard howls of laughter from the wolves.

Hap's stomach growled.

"I can't believe I dropped the steak," Hap muttered. "Now I have to go dig in the trash again. . . ."

The sun was rising. It would be hard to sneak into town now. Someone would see her.

Escaping from Lobo had worn her out. Hap needed to sleep. She walked to a nearby shrub.

"I'll just curl up and . . . " Hap tucked her nose under her paw. Before another moment could pass, she was dreaming. The dream she had been dreaming since she got lost:

A van is speeding down the highway. It pulls off at a gas station. The back doors of the van swing open. Dogs bark. Cage doors rattle. Hap's cage is the one closest to the rear doors. She can see the men talking. They are not paying attention. She can see the bigger man shut the first back door. Then he shuts the other, but it doesn't latch. The van lurches forward. It swerves. The unlatched door swings open. Hap feels her cage drift, then fly through space. She is trapped inside her cage. Her cage rolls and spins. Hap is facing the van as it pulls onto the highway. She sees the van's unlatched door swing shut. This time the latch catches. The van disappears. Hap throws herself against the side of the cage. The cage

rolls over. The door latch breaks. Hap crawls from the cage. She walks and walks. She meets animals who don't understand her. People aren't nice to her. Nothing is familiar. It's like being on the moon.

★ ★ ★ ★ ★ ★

"Arf!" Hap made a yipping sound when she woke.

One memory haunted her more than the rest. She saw the van driving away. The men wouldn't know Hap had been left behind until they counted the dogs. They might not do that until the end of the trip. That meant no one would search for her. And they wouldn't know where Hap had been lost.

I have to take care of myself now, thought Hap. She was trying to boost her confidence. *It's time to go find breakfast.*

Hap took the long way around to the garbage cans. It was safer.

Hap took a deep breath and rounded the corner. There were the trash cans. They looked full! Hap was careful not to lean too heavily on the cans. Knocking them over would be loud and make a mess.

What luck! There were half-eaten pancakes.
A pile of bacon, eggs, and potatoes. And
what was that other smell? Did someone have
sausages and eggs today and not clean their
plate?

Hap dug toward the wonderful smell of
sausage. She pulled away napkins, eggshells,
and plastic packaging. There was the sausage!

"*Grrr,*" she let out a soft, happy growl.

"Ha!" A voice thundered above her.

Two hands came around her neck. The sausage dropped from her mouth.

"At last!" It was a man's deep voice. "I got you!"

A rope tightened around Hap's neck.

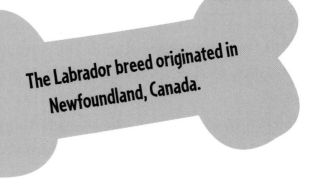

The Labrador breed originated in Newfoundland, Canada.

Caught!

15

Chapter 3

"**Y**ou made a mess of my trash cans!" said the man.

Hap tried to turn to see who was talking. But the rope was too tight.

"You're coming with me!" the man announced.

He dragged Hap to the front of the little restaurant. It was a small town. Hap could see one traffic light and about six buildings. There were only a few people walking around.

"Who do you have there, Lou?" asked a passerby.

"Stray! Just caught her out back. Want a dog?"

The passerby laughed.

"Last thing I need," said the passerby. "Another mouth to feed."

The man named Lou tied the other end of Hap's rope to a porch railing. Hap dropped her head. She thought of her family.

"You stay here while I figure out what to do with you!" Lou said. Hap looked him in the eye. The man paused.

"Do you have to look so sad?" Lou asked. He put his hands on his hips. Hap kept staring at him.

"Oh, all right!" he exclaimed. "I'll get you some water . . . and maybe just a little food."

Hap felt a wave a relief. She nudged her nose under Lou's hand. Lou laughed and gave her a pat.

"Well," he said, "aren't you something!"

Just then a young boy rushed up to Hap. "What a great-looking dog, Lou!" the boy cried. "When did you get her?"

"It's more like *she* got *me*!" Lou said.

An old man came up behind the boy.

"You want a dog, Old Luke?" Lou asked the old man.

Old Luke gave Hap a long look.

"Can we, Gramps?" begged the boy. He put an arm around Hap. "You've been saying we need a new dog!"

"Now hold on, Sean," Old Luke said to the boy. "We need a *sheepdog*. We don't need a pet!"

"I bet you'd be great with sheep! Wouldn't you, girl?" The boy looked Hap in the eye.

Hap didn't know what to think. She nuzzled under Sean's hand just like she had done to Lou.

"Aw, Gramps! Look! She likes me!"

"She's a smart one," Lou said. "You could do worse, Luke."

"You sure are," Sean whispered to Hap. "I can tell. You're real smart."

The boy scratched behind Hap's ears. He hugged her around the neck. Hap rested her head in his arms. It felt so good to have someone be nice to her again.

"Where'd she come from?" asked Old Luke.

"Just wandered up a week or so ago," Lou said. "I've been trying to catch her. I'm guessing she got dumped or lost. No doubt she belonged to someone. Look how friendly she is."

Hap wished as hard as she could for Sean to take her home. She wished for a big bowl of food.

"Never seen a Lab herd sheep before," Old Luke said.

"On the other hand"—Lou smiled—"she's the right price! Free! I'll even feed her a meal right now just to get you started!"

"Please, Gramps," Sean said. His voice was

quiet. He stared hard at his grandfather.

"If we take this dog home, Sean, it's not to be your pet," Old Luke said.

"I understand," Sean said.

But the boy nuzzled Hap. He whispered in her ear, "Don't you worry, girl. I'll take care of you!"

Hap licked Sean lightly on the hand.

★ ★ ★ ★ ★ ★

The road was bumpy. Hap was in the back of Old Luke's truck. It was a long ride. But Hap was feeling better. Lou had given her the best meal she'd had in a week. She tried to sit up in the back of the truck. But when she stood, she got knocked off her feet.

"Better sit down, girl!" Sean called. "The road just gets bumpier from here!"

Old Luke and the boy were in the cab of the truck. But Sean kept turning around to look at Hap and smile at her. Hap liked Sean, so she did as he said. She lay down.

It seemed like hours before the truck slowed down. At last Hap sat up. She looked all around.

She had never seen anything like this place. There was a big house and barns. There were three more trucks parked here and there.

"Welcome to the ranch!" Sean called to Hap. "Are we going to try her out with the sheep, Gramps?"

"Yes. Now hop out and go get the horses," Old Luke said.

The truck came to a stop. Sean ran toward one of the barns. He shouted to Hap, "Come on, girl. Get out of the truck!"

When Sean came back, he was leading two huge horses. Hap backed away. She'd never

seen a horse in person, only on TV.

That's the biggest animal I've ever seen! she thought.

"That's not a good sign," Old Luke snapped. "A herder afraid of horses?"

"You're not afraid, are you, girl?" Sean said. He stared at the dog. Hap understood. She had to work up her courage. She couldn't let Old Luke think she was scared.

"Just follow us, girl," Sean said. "It's a little ways yet."

Hap's feet were sore from her escape from Lobo. But she didn't let herself slow down. She kept pace with the horses. They walked and walked.

"Whoa!" Old Luke finally said.

The horses stopped. Hap looked up. She stepped out from behind the horses. Off in the distance were lots of white animals.

"There they are, girl," Sean said. "Meet the sheep!"

On their horses, Old Luke and Sean moved toward the flock of sheep.

The Right Job

Many dogs are bred to do certain jobs. But that doesn't mean they can't learn how to do new things. What matters is that a dog is intelligent. Some breeds are known to be smarter than others. German Shepherds, Labrador Retrievers, and Poodles are some of the smartest. Whether you're a person or a dog, a good brain helps you learn!

"Okay, dog," said Old Luke. "Prove to me that a Lab can be a sheepdog!"

Hap stepped away from the horses. She stared at the sheep. They stared back.

What does a sheepdog do? she wondered.

The sheep gathered together. As Hap stared at them, the flock began to whisper among themselves. It didn't take long for Hap to hear the first giggle.

Then it was like an explosion.

"DUCK DOG!" called the biggest sheep. "What do you want, Duck Dog?" The sheep roared in laughter.

Hap had a terrible feeling she was about to become a stray again.

Labs originally were bred to be sporting and waterfowl-hunting dogs.

Chapter 4

"Come on, girl," Sean called to Hap. "Get in there. Get the sheep moving. Get them back to the barn."

"Boy!" snapped Old Luke. "That kind of dog don't know how to herd. That's all there is to it. Dogs are bred to do things. This dog fetches

What do they want me to do?

ducks, not sheep."

"She could learn," Sean pleaded.

"A duck dog!" Old Luke exclaimed. "What was I thinking?"

"Everybody needs time when they're learning something new," Sean said. "Remember how long it took me to ride this horse? Now look at me!"

Hap knew she had to try. She stepped toward the sheep. They started to laugh again.

"*Quack!*" called the biggest sheep. "*Quack! Quack!*"

Hap ran into the middle of the flock. The sheep scattered.

"Oh, great!" called out Old Luke. "Now we got to herd them ourselves. Take the left flank, Sean. Don't let them scatter any farther."

Hap watched as Sean and Old Luke took charge. It was amazing. The two people knew how to circle around the sheep so they stayed together. First they gathered the sheep into a tight bunch. Then they got them to change direction. Finally, they started pushing the flock back toward the barns.

"See how that's done, Duck?" Old Luke said to Hap. "That's what I'm going to call you. Duck!"

Hap trotted behind the flock. She was between Sean and Old Luke.

"You named her!" Sean exclaimed. "That means we get to keep her!"

"It means I'll give you two weeks to turn her into a sheepdog. If you can do that, you can keep her. If you can't, she will have to find another home."

"Okay!" Sean shouted.

The boy looked at Hap. Hap wished she could leap up and lick his cheek. He was a wonderful boy!

"*I'll do whatever you say!*" Hap barked. "*I promise!*"

"Okay, Duck," said Sean. "It's up to us!"

★ ★ ★ ★ ★ ★

Hap sat patiently in the corner of the barn. Sean and Old Luke were tending to the sheep. They had to be put in pens, then fed. Hap admired how much Sean knew. He was a smart boy.

When they were done, Old Luke headed toward the house.

"Hurry up with the rest of your chores," he said to Sean. "Your mother will have dinner on the table in five minutes."

"Yes, sir," Sean said.

Hap stood up. She trotted over to Sean. She had been waiting all this time to say thank you. She stood next to the boy and leaned against his leg. When he knelt down, she licked his face. Sean laughed.

"Okay, okay, Duck." He giggled. "I'll get you your dinner. But first I want you to meet somebody."

Sean walked toward one of the pens where the sheep were resting. Hap followed him.

"Stay here," Sean said to Hap.

The boy climbed over the fence. He made his way into the middle of the sheep.

Baaaaa! Baaa! The sheep scattered and complained.

Sean put his hands on the biggest sheep. It was the sheep who had been so mean to Hap in the field.

"This is Ewe," said Sean to Hap. "And just so you know, that's a joke. A female sheep is called a ewe, so Gramps thought it would be funny to name one Ewe."

"Insulting!" Hap heard the sheep mutter.

Sheep complain a lot, thought Hap.

Sean pulled Ewe away from the other sheep. He introduced them.

"Duck, this is Ewe."

"Duck Dog," baaed Ewe.

"You don't have to be mean," Hap said quietly.

"Ewe is the leader of the sheep, Duck," Sean explained. "You have to get to know her. If you can get Ewe to trust you, then the rest of them will follow."

"Fat chance," Ewe muttered.

Hap looked at Sean. She tried not to look worried. But Sean could tell she was nervous.

"Don't worry, girl," Sean said. He knelt

Traditional Sheepdogs

Many dog breeds have worked as sheepdogs. Border Collies, Koolies (an Australian breed), and English Shepherd Dogs are just a few of those breeds. They do their job by running around and nipping at the animals they are herding. Some sheepdogs use the "strong eye." That means they stand in front of a sheep and stare at it until the sheep does what the dog wants. Border Collies are best known for "strong eye."

down and scratched behind her ears. "Everything is going to be okay."

Sean headed toward the house. Ewe waited for the barn door to close behind him. Then she stepped closer to Hap.

"Don't even try it! Who do you think we are? We don't even trust dogs who *know* what they're doing! Why should we trust *you*? Sheep aren't stupid. We know dogs are basically wolves. And who do you think you're supposed to protect us from, Duck Dog? WOLVES! That's who!"

Hap could feel her legs turn to jelly.

"Wolves?" she repeated.

"Yes!" cried Ewe. "You're supposed to protect us from wolves!"

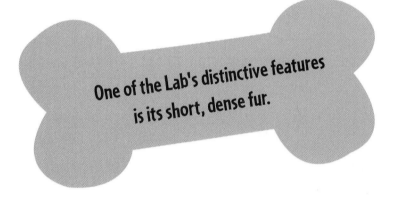

One of the Lab's distinctive features is its short, dense fur.

Chapter 5

"**G**ood morning, Duck!" Sean called.

Hap was pulled from a sound sleep. She lifted her head. It was still dark outside.

Morning comes early on the ranch! she thought.

"Time to get up!" Sean said.

She felt a pair of hands gently ruffle her ears. Sean leaned down next to her. "You've got a big job today, Duck. We have to show Gramps that you're making progress!"

"*Woof!*" Hap barked softly. She followed Sean around the barn as he did his chores. She stopped following him when he set her breakfast down. She couldn't help it. She had to devour the food.

"Settle down, girl." Sean laughed. "You're not starving anymore."

Hap heard Sean. But she still had the fear of a stray dog. She had to eat whatever she could. She had to eat food as soon as she found it.

★ ★ ★ ★ ★ ★

"Let's head out!" Old Luke called.

The sun was rising quickly. Hap trotted alongside the sheep. She watched Sean carefully. She had no idea what she was supposed to do. Only Sean would be able to help her. She could feel Old Luke's eyes on her. He was waiting for her to mess up.

When's dinner?

Ewe appeared at the edge of the flock. She walked along right next to Hap.

"Have you been thinking about those wolves, Duck Dog?" the big sheep asked Hap. "Have you figured out how to keep us safe from them?"

The other sheep chuckled. They waited for Hap to answer Ewe's question. Hap knew she had to hide her fear of wolves. The sheep must not see her afraid.

"You think I've never faced wolves before?" Hap asked. She tried to look confident. "I was a stray! I survived out there on my own!"

"Good," said Ewe, "because there's one over there!"

Hap couldn't stop herself. She jumped and spun around. She yelped.

The sheep exploded in laughter. There was no wolf. Ewe had fooled her.

"What's wrong, girl?" Sean called to Hap.

"Stop upsetting the sheep, Duck!" Old Luke snapped.

Hap hung her head. She couldn't look at

Ewe. She was getting mad now. She had to figure out how to handle these sheep. They were going to be sorry they picked on her.

"This is it!" announced Old Luke. "Keep them in line, Duck!"

Sean got down off his horse. He moved quickly to Hap's side.

"That means we're going to graze the sheep in this field today, Duck," Sean said. "So you have to keep them from wandering away. You can do that, can't you?"

I wouldn't mind losing a few of these sheep, thought Hap.

She glared at Ewe. She turned back to Sean.

"*Woof!*" she said loudly.

Just then, Ewe shouted at all the sheep, "Scatter!"

All the sheep headed in different directions. Hap froze. She had no idea what to do. She chased after one, but that made them scatter even more. She headed after two who were headed to the creek. Then she changed direction and went after three who were headed back to the barns.

"No! No!" shouted Old Luke. "The dog doesn't even know how to circle. This is pointless."

Sean ran after Hap. He pulled her away from the sheep.

"I don't understand!" Hap barked.

"You keep them together by running around the outside of the flock," Sean told her.

"I'm going for the ones that ran to the barn," Old Luke called. The old man turned his horse around. He headed back toward the barns.

Sean ran with Hap. They made a wide circle around the sheep. Little by little, the sheep came back together. Finally, they were under control. Sean stopped running.

Suddenly, an unfamiliar voice rang out.

"Who's the dog, Baaa Boy? You or that furry yellow thing?"

Hap turned to see three boys watching. They looked older than Sean.

"Oh, great," Sean muttered. "The meanest

boys in the state," he whispered to Hap.

Hap looked for Old Luke. If only the old man would come back.

"If you're a dog, maybe we should tie a rope around you and make sure you don't run away!"

The boys laughed harder. They stepped toward Sean. Hap let out a low growl. She wasn't sure how to protect sheep from wolves, but she knew how to make these bullies stop picking on Sean. Hap stepped toward Sean. She had to get in front of him. But then something strange happened. Sean started screeching. His arms flew around. He fell to the ground. He kicked his legs. He was moving so fast, it was hard to tell what was happening.

The boys froze in their tracks.

"What's wrong with you?" one shouted.

Sean almost stood up, but then his legs started kicking again. He was out of control.

"Something's wrong with him!" another boy cried. "Let's get out of here before we get blamed!"

Kids and Dogs

People have been attached to dogs for a long time. Dogs are good companions. They protect us. They do jobs for us. But kids and dogs seem to just like each other for who they are. Maybe that's why so many great books have been written about kids and dogs. Have you read *Shiloh, Old Yeller,* or *Where the Red Fern Grows?*

The three bullies turned and ran. In no time, they had disappeared. Sean suddenly stopped moving. Hap rushed to his side. His eyes were closed.

Hap licked his face. Slowly, Sean's eyes opened. He started to smile.

"The old crazy act, girl." He laughed. "It works every time!"

"You're a genius!" Hap barked. *What a smart boy*, she thought.

Hap and Sean rolled around on the ground together. They were laughing and shouting. Hap hadn't felt this good in weeks.

"What in tarnation?" Old Luke's voice thundered. "Boy! Have you forgotten everything I taught you?"

Hap and Sean stopped. They looked at Old Luke. Then Hap looked at the sheep, who had scattered again.

"I'm sorry," Hap cried. "I'll get them."

"Get over here, boy!" Old Luke snapped. "I told you that dog is not a pet!"

Hap ran in circles. She did everything she could to round up the sheep. But Ewe was working against her.

"Go left!" Ewe shouted when they were almost gathered.

Hap tried again. Once again, she almost got them into a group. But then Ewe baaed, "Run to the barns!"

It's hopeless, thought Hap. *I can't do anything if Ewe is my enemy!*

She stole a glance at Old Luke. She wondered if he understood that Ewe was the problem. But Old Luke was still scolding Sean.

"This is not going to work!" Hap heard him say. "The dog goes back! We need a real sheepdog!"

Chapter 6

Hap stood in the field with the sheep. Sean and Old Luke sat in the truck. Its doors were open so the air could move. Two days had passed since Old Luke said Hap had to go. Hap wondered how much longer she would get to stay. But Sean had not given up. He begged his grandfather daily. He had tried again this morning. They were all headed to the fields.

"Please, Gramps," Sean cried. "Don't find her a new home! She is getting better. You just haven't seen it. Besides, the sheep are being really bad. It's not all Duck's fault. They've been trying to get away just to cause trouble."

But every time Sean begged, Old Luke got more certain. Hap must go.

"Boy!" Old Luke said to Sean. "You are about to push me round the bend. Now stop asking me the same thing over and over!"

"Nice knowing you, Duck Dog!" Ewe was talking to Hap in a low voice. "Hope you find something to retrieve soon!"

The rest of the sheep burst into laughter. Hap wanted to get even with the sheep. But she was too sad to be mean. She hung her head.

Sean slid down from the truck seat. His head hung almost as low as Hap's.

"Where you going, boy?" Old Luke asked.

"I'm going to take a walk," Sean murmured. Actually, he thought he might cry. He wanted to be alone.

"I'll make sure it's a good home," Old Luke said. The old man was trying to make Sean feel better. "We'll make sure Duck's okay."

Hap lifted her head. It broke her heart. She had to do something. She turned to Ewe.

"Look!" Hap said to the sheep. "We are going to work this out!"

Ewe looked shocked. The old sheep was silent. Hap was amazed. Suddenly, they were listening to her. But before she could say anything, a terrible *SNAP!* rang out.

"OWWW!" Sean screamed. He was hidden by a small group of trees.

Old Luke and Hap raced toward the boy. It was a terrible sight. Sean was on the ground, curled up in pain. A big rusty metal trap was clamped to his ankle. His pant leg was covered in blood.

What happened to Sean?

"Sean!" Hap barked. She licked his face.

"Hang on, boy," Old Luke said. He sounded scared. Old Luke studied the ankle. "I'm not going to remove the trap, Sean," his grandfather explained. "I think it might be holding some broken bones in place.

We'll get you to the doctor, and he'll do it."

Sean moaned. Hap stood back. Her heart was pounding. She wanted to jump in the truck with Sean. But Old Luke looked back at her.

"It's up to you, Duck. I need you to take care of the sheep." Old Luke set Sean down gently on the truck seat.

"Sean!" Hap barked.

"I'll take care of the boy," Old Luke said sternly. "You take care of the sheep."

Hap stood quiet and still. She watched the truck drive away. It disappeared. She turned back to the sheep. They looked as scared as she felt.

Hap took a deep breath. She had to be brave. She had to be tough. She had to be smart.

"Old Luke will take care of Sean," Hap whispered to herself. She tried to calm down. "Sean will be fine." She said the words to herself over and over.

The sun began to set. Darkness stretched across the ranch. The sheep were quieter than Hap had ever seen them.

Tonight, nobody wanted any trouble. It got darker and scarier.

Brave. Tough. Smart. Brave. Tough. Smart. Hap chanted the words to herself. She circled the sheep slowly. She kept her nose to the air. She kept her ears pricked. Wolves could appear at any minute. It might just be the sound of

Dogs in the Dark
Dogs do lots of things better than people do. They smell better. They have better hearing. During the day, they *don't* see as well. However, at night, dogs see better than people do! Their eyes are built to need less light. Dogs also have better peripheral vision, which means they can see farther to the side. So if you're trying to find your way in the dark . . . bring along a dog!

a pebble rolling. Or maybe the sound of a snapping twig.

Or—Hap froze. So did the sheep. Rustling grass. They all heard it.

Something was out there.

The Lab is a member of the sporting group of dog breeds.

Chapter 7

The sheep tightened their flock. Hap could hear them whimpering. She stood in one spot and turned in a full circle. She studied the dark edges around the flock.

She barked.

"Yellow-belly!" hissed an oily voice.

Hap was staring right into the yellow eyes of Lobo. He was so close.

"Who was dumb enough to put *you* in charge of a juicy flock of sheep?" Lobo laughed.

The other wolves laughed with him.

Hap could feel the fear rising in the sheep. She could tell they were working hard not to run. Hap understood. She wanted to run, too. But they were all trying to stay calm. Hap knew it wouldn't last. She had to rescue them. Old Luke was counting on her. Sean was counting on her. The sheep were counting on her.

She had to chase away the wolves. She had to do it before the sheep scattered. If they scattered, Hap could never protect them all.

She counted the wolves behind Lobo. It was a bigger pack than the first time Hap met them. There were at least seven.

"You don't really think you can protect all these sheep from us, do you?" Lobo asked Hap. He smiled a terrible smile.

"Save us!" Hap heard a voice behind her. "I'm sorry." Hap realized it was Ewe. She was begging Hap to help and apologizing for how she had behaved.

"I'm going to do you a favor, yellow-belly," Lobo said. "You can choose which sheep we get. It's a perfect plan. We don't have to tire ourselves out. The sheep don't have to hurt themselves running in fear. And you don't have to prove how hopeless you are as a sheepdog."

Hap lowered her head to the ground. Her fear was turning to anger.

"Okay," hissed Lobo. "If you don't want to

do it our way—STRIKE!" Lobo commanded his wolves.

Dogs on Guard!
Throughout history, dogs have been used to guard things. Humans have depended on dogs to guard homes, barns, horses, land, sheep, cows, and just about anything else of value. Most breeds of dog will guard their people and territory. But certain breeds are better at it than others. Two good examples of guard dogs are Dobermans and Rottweilers.

It all happened so fast. Three wolves leaped into the flock. The sheep screamed in terror. They scattered in every direction. The rest of the wolves howled. Lobo's high-pitched laugh hurt Hap's ears. But then Hap heard a noise that was even worse.

"H-E-E-L-L-P!" It was a cry of pain. One of the sheep had been attacked.

Hap was done thinking. She was done being scared. She couldn't let Sean down.

Sean! It was like she was struck by lightning. She suddenly realized she knew what to do. Sean had given her the answer!

I can do it!

Hap leaped right into the middle of the wolves. She let out a screaming howl more frightening than any wolf howl. Hap jumped up on her back legs. She spun herself in circles. Her tongue hung out of her mouth. She made growling sounds. Then she yelped a bunch of fast-paced yips and yaps. She fell on the ground and slithered like a snake. She jumped back on her feet. She flung herself sideways into half the wolves.

"UGH!" gasped one wolf.

"What's wrong with that dog?" screamed Lobo's second-in-command.

"It looks like she has rabies!" called another.

"Stop it, yellow-belly!" Lobo commanded.

But Hap only acted crazier. She looked more and more wild.

"Rabies?" the wolves called to one another.

"Rabies!" they shouted in fear.

The attack ended as quickly as it had begun. The wolves ran away from the "crazy dog" as fast as they could.

"They're gone!" Hap exclaimed. She couldn't believe she'd chased them away. "I did it! The old crazy act!"

Hap looked at the sheep. They weren't smiling. They didn't look happy. Why not?

"H-e-e-l-l-p . . ."

Hap heard the same cry she had heard before. But now it was weaker. She ran to the sheep.

Ewe lay on the ground. She was perfectly still, bright red blood staining her white coat.

Chapter 8

"Ewe," Hap whispered. "Come on! Wake up! Wake up!"

The big sheep slowly opened her eyes. She moaned.

"You're going to be okay," said Hap.

She wanted the sheep to believe her. But she didn't believe herself. How was she going to save the leader of the flock? If Hap left them to get help, the wolves might come back. If she didn't get help . . . she couldn't think about it.

"Talk to me, Ewe. Just stay awake." Hap was remembering things she'd heard on TV. She used to watch TV with her old family.

Ewe looked at Hap. She looked so confused.

"What were you like when you were a young sheep?" asked Hap. "Tell me something about your mom and dad."

Hap looked at the other sheep. Couldn't someone help? They all looked too scared to talk. Hap heard a terrible rasping sound. She realized it was Ewe trying to breathe.

"I was the first born to my mother," Ewe whispered.

Hap slowly lay down. She put her ear close to the sheep's mouth.

"Yes?" Hap said.

"I'm from a long line, you know," Ewe said. She looked Hap in the eye. Hap thought she looked a little proud. "Old Luke's first sheep . . ."

"Wow," whispered Hap. "I didn't know that."

"My great-great-great-grandmother . . ." Ewe gasped.

Hap could tell she was in a lot of pain. Hap licked her face. The sheep sighed.

"She was given to Old Luke to pay a debt. . . ."

"Somebody used your grandmother as

money?" Hap was amazed.

Ewe looked at Hap. She blinked and gave a little nod.

"That seems wrong," said Hap.

"Yes," Ewe agreed.

"Families are supposed to stick together," Hap said.

"Sometimes old families have to be left behind," whispered Ewe.

Hap cocked her head. Pictures of *her* old family passed through her mind. Then she pictured Sean's face. She took a deep breath.

Sean will be fine, she told herself. She turned back to Ewe.

"You're right," Hap whispered. "I used to have another family, too."

They stared at each other. Ewe seemed to almost smile.

Hap understood now. If she wanted a new family, she had to let go of the old one. This was her chance. She had to be a sheepdog now. She had to do it for Sean and Old Luke and Ewe.

Best Friends!

There is an old saying: "A dog is man's best friend." It's true that lots of people and dogs are best friends. But they are not the only case of different species being best friends. Owen and Mzee, a hippo and a tortoise from Kenya, had a book written about them. A German Shepherd named Hazel likes it when an owl named Boobah rides on her head. The pair have made headlines around the world!

"Aauugghh . . ." Ewe's eyes were closing.

She was getting weaker.

Hap stood up. She looked at the other sheep.

"We have to get Ewe back to the barn!" Hap told them. "We can do it, but you have to do as I say!"

Hap stared hard at the sheep. She couldn't tell what they were thinking. Would they listen to her?

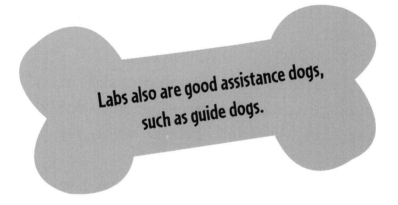

Labs also are good assistance dogs, such as guide dogs.

Chapter 9

Hap stared at Ewe. She was a big sheep. Hap closed her eyes. She tried to imagine getting her back to the barn.

"We have to carry her," Hap said.

A murmur rose from the sheep. They were talking to one another. But they were talking softly. Hap couldn't hear what they were saying.

"We have to do this," Hap said.

She tried to sound strong. But she knew she sounded scared. The sheep began to surround Ewe. Hap couldn't believe what she was seeing.

Some of the sheep lay down next to Ewe. They gently rolled themselves toward her. They carefully pushed themselves underneath her. Slowly the big sheep was propped up.

Other sheep stood around her to support her weight. The sheep on the ground struggled to their feet. Ewe was almost on their backs. More sheep wiggled in next to them. They lifted the rest of Ewe up onto their backs.

Hap's mouth dropped open. The sheep had made themselves into a bed! They stood close to one another. They began to walk carefully. They were carrying Ewe on their backs!

"Brilliant!" Hap cried out.

The rest of the sheep gathered around Ewe. They moved as a team. Ewe was safe in the middle of them.

"I'll guard you against the wolves," Hap announced. "I promise!"

They began the journey back to the barn. Hap circled around the sheep. She never stopped moving. Her eyes never stopped searching the darkness.

She searched for Old Luke. What was keeping him? Was Sean in more trouble than they thought?

Hap cleared the worries from her head.

She had a job to do. She had to stay focused. She guarded the sheep. She felt proud to be part of this family.

The Truth about Sheep

A strong instinct in sheep is to flock together. This behavior has made some people believe that sheep are not smart. But the truth is that scientists have determined they are as smart as cows and almost as smart as pigs. Sheep can learn to recognize a person's face and then remember that face even after many years!

"You're doing a great job," Hap told them. "Just hang in there!"

But then Lobo's voice broke through the darkness. "You're walking away with my dinner!" the wolf said with a sneer.

Hap and the sheep froze.

"That sheep is mine!" Lobo growled.

Hap circled the sheep. She found Lobo's eyes in the darkness. The wolf was alone. He had come back to face Hap on his own.

This time Hap didn't hesitate. She lifted her head and opened her mouth. She howled a bloodcurdling scream. Then she ran, faster than she had ever run. She ran directly at Lobo. Her scream filled the air as she charged into the wolf. She knocked into him like a bulldozer. He fell, rolling three times. Hap heard him yelp. But she didn't stop. Lobo struggled back to his feet. But Hap was on him again. She crashed into the wolf. This time her teeth sank into the wolf's ear. Lobo cried in pain. He landed hard on the ground.

Hap circled fast. She was going to charge him again. But Lobo turned away. His tail was tucked between his legs. He ran into the darkness. Hap followed him. She howled even louder. She ran until she was sure Lobo was gone.

Finally, she stopped running. She was standing in absolute darkness.

I did it, she thought. *I saved the family!*

But she didn't have time to dwell on the good feeling. She had to get Ewe to help. She had to make sure Sean was okay.

Hap ran back to the sheep. When she reached them, she stopped in her tracks.

The sheep were all facing her. They let out a soft *baa*. Then all the sheep bowed their heads in thanks.

"We're a good team," Hap said shyly. "Now let's go. There's not much time left."

They began to move. Hap realized dawn was breaking. A sliver of light was appearing at the horizon. She looked at Ewe on top of the sheep. Hap could tell Ewe was shivering badly.

Just then, she saw headlights. A truck was coming toward them. Hap realized the outline of the barn was just beyond the truck.

"We made it!" she shouted. "Ewe, you're going to be okay!"

She turned back to Ewe. The sheep had stopped walking. Ewe was not shivering anymore. She was completely still.

Old Luke jumped down from the truck. He was alone.

"Where is Sean?" Hap barked.

Old Luke stood silent.

Hap looked from Ewe to Old Luke. Her heart was breaking.

We've lost them both! she thought.

She lifted her head and howled at the fading moon.

Chapter 10

Suddenly, Old Luke broke into a run. He didn't stop when he reached the flock. He saw Ewe and scooped her up in his arms.

"Save her!" Hap barked.

Old Luke turned and stared at Hap. He had a funny look on his face. Hap couldn't tell what he was thinking.

I did the best I could, Hap thought.

But she felt sad. Her head dropped. Old Luke rushed away.

Baaa. The sheep gathered around Hap. They bleated softly.

"Okay," Hap said quietly. "Follow me to the gate."

Hap moved slowly toward the gate that led to the sheep's stalls. She stepped to the side when she reached the gate. The sheep moved

in a neat line. They stepped right through the gate without argument. Hap watched them walk. She realized how happy this would have made her a day ago. But now everything had changed. Now she couldn't feel good about anything.

Hap heard shuffling feet behind her. She turned. Old Luke was standing just outside the barn. Hap thought she couldn't bear what he might have to say.

"Come here, girl!" he said. A small smile broke across his face.

How can you look happy? Hap thought.

She turned around and looked behind her. She didn't know who Old Luke was talking to.

"You, Duck! I'm talking to you."

Hap stared in disbelief.

"Come here, girl. You are a good dog! You are a *very* good dog!"

Hap stepped slowly toward Old Luke. She felt like she was dreaming.

"I've never seen anything like that," Old Luke said to Hap. "I've never seen an injured sheep get rescued like that."

Hap stood in front of Old Luke. She looked him in the eye. He bent and ruffled her ears. He gave her a good pat on the side.

"Duck!" another voice called to her.

Hap turned around. Sean was standing at the door of the house. His leg was wrapped in a big white bandage. He was on crutches. Hap broke into a run. She raced to her boy.

"Are you okay?" she barked to Sean. "Does it hurt?"

She reached the boy and slowed down. She knew she had to be careful. He was badly injured.

"Pretty fancy leg, eh, Duck?" Sean laughed.

Hap nuzzled him gently. She sat right at his side.

"Your dog saved the sheep," shouted Old Luke to his grandson. "Thanks to her, we still got Ewe!"

Hap couldn't believe her ears. Ewe was alive! Everyone was going to be okay!

Sean eased himself down the front steps of the house. He sat down slowly. Then he put his arms around Hap's neck.

"I told you!" Sean whispered. "I knew you could do it!"

Hap buried her head in Sean's lap. She had never been happier to see someone in her whole life. Finally, she lifted her head and licked him on the face. Sean threw back his head and laughed.

"So what do you say now, Gramps?" asked Sean. "May we keep her?"

Old Luke studied the pair. But he said nothing. After a minute he gave a single nod. Then he went back into the barn.

Hap barked just because she felt so happy. Sean hugged her one more time. Then Hap stood up. She gave

Sean a loving look. Then she turned away.

"Where are you going, girl?" Sean asked.

Hap trotted toward the barn. She had another friend she had to check on.

Ewe lay quietly on a bed of hay. Old Luke was still cleaning her wound. But her breathing was even. Her eyes were open. Hap stepped to her side. She put her nose to Ewe's head. She nudged her gently.

Ewe murmured a quiet *baaa*.

"How are you, my friend?" asked Hap.

"I'll be fine," Ewe whispered. She looked at the dog. She gave Hap a grateful nod.

Hap heard Sean come into the barn.

"Don't push yourself, boy," Old Luke said. "It will be a while before the leg heals."

"Me and Ewe are some pair!" Sean laughed. "Good thing we've got Duck!"

Old Luke stood and looked at Hap.

"Turns out she's a sheepdog, huh, Gramps?" Sean said.

"Best sheepdog I ever owned," Old Luke said plainly.

Sean and Old Luke were quiet for a minute.
Then they burst out laughing. Ewe bleated in
agreement.

Hap sat quietly. She looked at the sheep and

at Old Luke and Sean. Then she leaped to her feet. She couldn't stop herself. She loved this family, and it was hers!

Labs are the number one most registered dog breed in the United States and many other countries.